Cheerleading

Cheer Professionals

Cheer as a Career

by Jen Jones

Consultant

Lindsay Evered-Ceilley

Former Denver Broncos Cheerleader and Denver Nuggets Dancer

Director of Business Operations,
Centerstage Starz Theatre and Dance Studio
Centennial, Colorado

Capstone press®

Mankato, Minnesota

Snap Books are published by Capstone Press,
151 Good Counsel Drive, P.O. Box 669, Mankato, Minnesota 56002.
www.capstonepress.com

Library of Congress Cataloging-in-Publication data

Jones, Jen.

   Cheer professionals: Cheer as a career / by Jen Jones.

   p. cm. — (Snap books. Cheerleading)

   Summary: "Upbeat text provides an in-depth look at cheer professionals,
describes their activities, opportunities, skills, and demands, and profiles top pro
squads" — Provided by publisher.

   Includes bibliographical references and index.

   ISBN-13: 978-1-4296-1349-1 (hardcover)

   ISBN-10: 1-4296-1349-1 (hardcover)

   1. Dance teams — Juvenile literature. 2. Cheerleading — Juvenile literature.
I. Title. II. Series.

GV1798.J66 2008

791.6'4 — dc22   2007018176

Editorial Credits

Jenny Marks, editor; Kim Brown, designer; Jo Miller, photo researcher

Photo Credits

AP Images/Bill Kostroun, 7; Matt York, 23; Mel Evans, 15

Getty Images Inc./Bob Berg, 25 (left) ; Jonathan Daniel, 19; NBAE/Bill Baptist, 9; NBAE/Glenn James, 18; NBAE/Kent Smith, 16–17; NBAE
    Melissa Majchrzak, 21; NBAE/Rocky Widner, 5; NBAE/Terrance Vaccaro, 28–29; Paul Spinelli, 27

Jamie Christian Photography, 11

Michele Torma Lee, 32

ZUMA Press/Icon SMI/James D. Smith, cover; Icon Sports Media, 25 (right); Palm Beach Post/Gary Coronado, 13

1 2 3 4 5 6 13 12 11 10 09 08

Table of Contents

Cheer through Your Years

Who says you have to hang up your pom-poms after college? Cheerleading can truly be a lifelong pursuit. Cheer camps, pro sports leagues, and all-star gyms are full of cheer opportunities. From dancing for 30,000 fans to coaching champions, the world of pro cheer has a place for you!

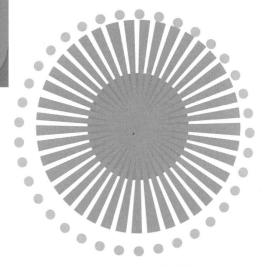

"Prepare for professional success!"

This book sheds light on the many avenues for going pro. Yes, this means getting paid to cheer! From auditions to games, you'll learn what it's really like to be in the big leagues. And you'll uncover what launched several pro squads into cheer fame. Prepare for professional success!

Movin' on up to the Big Time

Just like the pro sports teams they support, pro cheerleaders are top athletes. Pro cheer teams span the sports world, from basketball to hockey. Even international sports teams have caught pro cheer spirit. Squads have popped up in the Canadian Football League, the NFL Europa, and the Korean Baseball League.

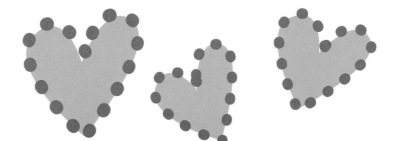

Pro cheerleading is a far cry from high school and college squads. Many teams are strictly dance-oriented and require advanced dance skills. Cheerleaders get paid for their work and receive perks. Typical pay might be anywhere from $40 to $80 per game, and $10 to $30 per practice. Plus, pro cheerleaders are celebrities in their own right. They get to strut their stuff in the public eye!

Crowd Pleasers

Although dance teams are poplar, many sports teams are looking at the big picture. Their cheer departments expand to add even more crowd appeal. Stunt and tumble teams, breakdancers, and dunk teams are added to the mix. They complement the dance team, adding spice and sizzle. Most importantly, they pump up the crowd. It's all about well-rounded entertainment.

Some alternative teams leading the way include:

Milwaukee Bucks Rim Rocker Dunk Team: Watch as these jumpin' acrobats flip and dunk to get the crowd on their feet.

Detroit Pistons Work Force: This high-flying, coed cheer squad performs amazing stunts and tumbling.

Denver Broncos Stampede: Crowds groove to the rhythm of this peppy 12-member drumline.

Utah Jazz Jr. Jazz Dancers: This group of young dancers has big talent.

What's the best part of all this growth in pro cheer? Now even more people can get in the game.

CKETS

All-Stars for Life

Who says your all-star sparkle dims as an adult? Open all-star squads make it possible to cheer long after high school. Members must be age 18 or older. And all those years of experience show on the floor. Competing at Level 6, open teams play by rules that allow advanced stunts and tumbling. From helicopter tosses to towering 2 ½ high pyramids, open cheer takes all-star competition to a new level.

Another trend is the growing number of parent teams. In a *Freaky Friday*-style scenario, parents of all-stars join forces to see what cheering is really like. Some competitions even add divisions for parent teams, with quite entertaining results! Picture dozens of parents hamming it up for the crowd. Who could blame them? After all, kids shouldn't get to have all the fun. There's plenty to go around!

"Shake It 'Til You Make It!"

Camping Out

Why spend your summer working an average job? Being a cheer camp instructor is the way to go! Instructors travel from camp to camp all summer. They stay at college campuses around the country. Perks include making new friends, staying in shape, and teaching thousands of cheerleaders. Best of all, they get paid to do what they love.

Of course, landing the job isn't easy. Wannabe instructors must try out against other top college cheerleaders. Star quality is essential to stand apart from the pack. Another way in is to get "apped" while attending camp. Talented high school seniors are sometimes offered job applications to submit once they are in college. For those who make the cut, an unforgettable summer awaits!

"An unforgettable summer awaits!"

13

Behind the Scenes

Camp instructor and pro cheerleader are great jobs. But some athletes want to give their bodies a break. Others are just ready to try something new. Enter coaching and choreography! These jobs allow cheerleaders to apply their cheer knowledge and earn money for it.

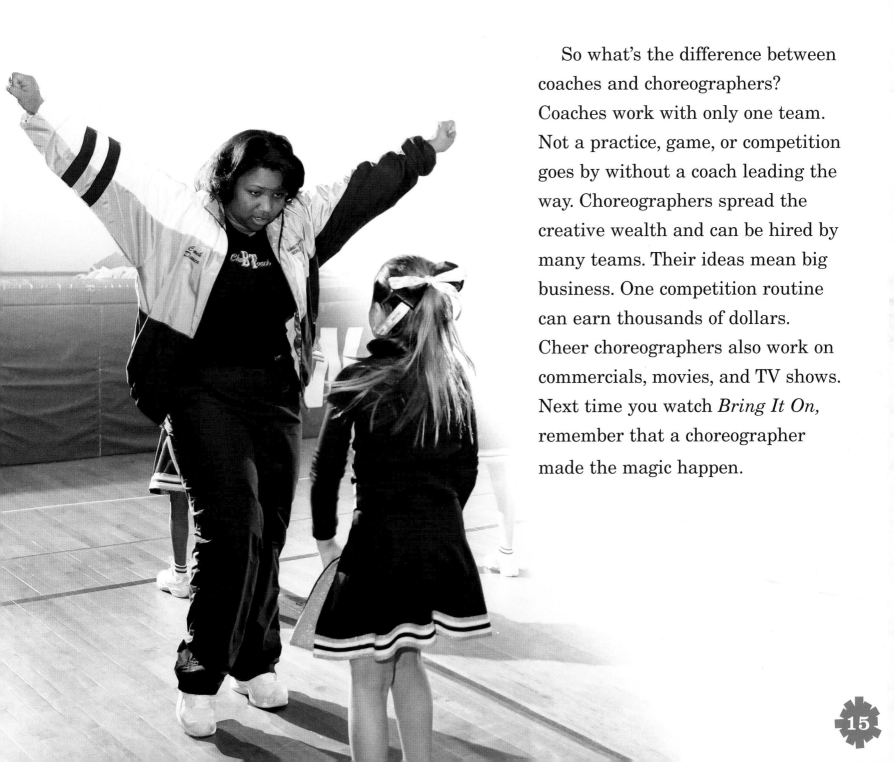

So what's the difference between coaches and choreographers? Coaches work with only one team. Not a practice, game, or competition goes by without a coach leading the way. Choreographers spread the creative wealth and can be hired by many teams. Their ideas mean big business. One competition routine can earn thousands of dollars. Cheer choreographers also work on commercials, movies, and TV shows. Next time you watch *Bring It On,* remember that a choreographer made the magic happen.

One in a Million

Thousands of women dream of cheering for pro sports teams. But only a select few get the chance. Most sports teams are based in big cities with a large pool of talented dancers. Tryouts attract hundreds or even thousands of women. Returning cheerleaders must also audition to keep their spots. The competition is stiff!

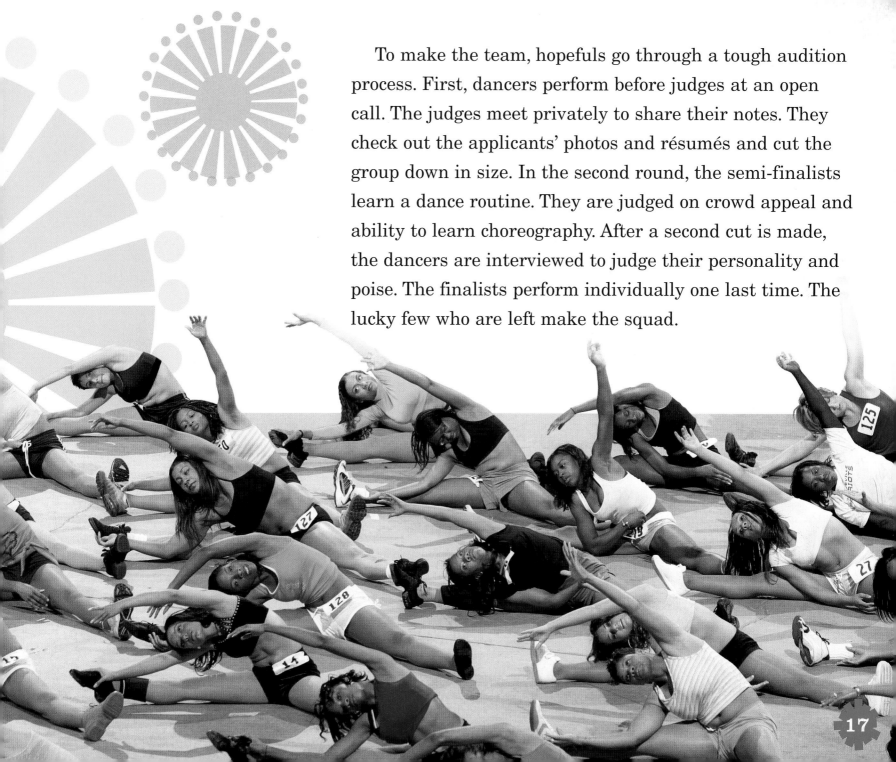

To make the team, hopefuls go through a tough audition process. First, dancers perform before judges at an open call. The judges meet privately to share their notes. They check out the applicants' photos and résumés and cut the group down in size. In the second round, the semi-finalists learn a dance routine. They are judged on crowd appeal and ability to learn choreography. After a second cut is made, the dancers are interviewed to judge their personality and poise. The finalists perform individually one last time. The lucky few who are left make the squad.

The Right Stuff

Only the best make it to the big leagues, and pro cheer is no different. Those who make the squad must display the right mix of spirit, talent, and style. During auditions, judges and coaches look for the following:

Athleticism: Is the cheerleader trained in different styles of dance? Can she perform turns, leaps, and jumps? For a non-dance team, are stunts and tumbling moves performed well?

Appearance: Does the cheerleader make an effort to look her best? Does she seem to have a sense of style and a big, beaming smile?

Personality: Does the cheerleader show spirit and confidence while performing? Will her showmanship project into a stadium full of thousands?

Poise: Does she carry herself with grace and dignity? Will she represent the team well at public appearances and interviews?

19

Business as Usual

Huge arenas, blinding lights, and scores of screaming fans. Sounds like the life of a rock star, right? It's also the glamorous life of a pro cheerleader!

For most sports, cheerleaders are at the center of it all. During a game, the squad entertains at time-outs, between quarters, and during the occasional halftime. If the game is shown on TV, these fabulous gals might snag on-screen close-ups!

Yet pro cheer isn't all glitz and glory. Cheerleaders treat their place on the squad like a part-time job. Practices and rehearsals are typically held at least twice a week. All are expected to attend. On game days, cheerleaders are on the scene several hours before the big show. Sometimes they make official post-game appearances as well.

Pro cheerleaders get paid for their hard work. But they also receive perks. Free gym memberships, tanning, and hair care are all part of the pro-cheer package. No doubt, pro cheer is a one-of-a-kind employment!

Spreading Cheer

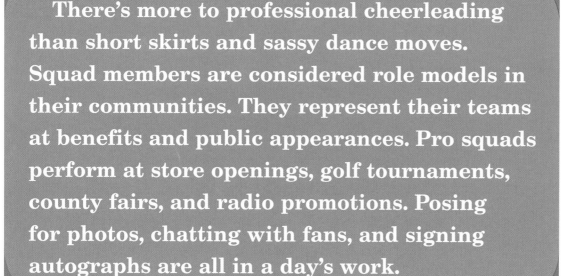

There's more to professional cheerleading than short skirts and sassy dance moves. Squad members are considered role models in their communities. They represent their teams at benefits and public appearances. Pro squads perform at store openings, golf tournaments, county fairs, and radio promotions. Posing for photos, chatting with fans, and signing autographs are all in a day's work.

For many, the most rewarding part of professional cheerleading is charity and outreach work. Squads often visit hospitals, schools, and military bases. They spread cheer to those who need it most.

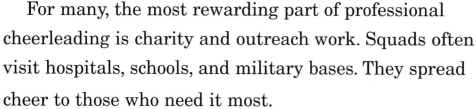

Pro cheerleaders also raise money for causes close to their hearts. Common charity fund-raisers include dance marathons, car washes, and fashion shows. Doing good deeds is part of the job description.

THE STUFF THAT LEGENDS ARE MADE OF

You Go, Laker Girls!

What bleeds purple and gold and loves to dance? A Laker Girl, of course!

The Laker Girls are one of pro cheer's legendary teams. A major reason for their rise to fame is the success of the Los Angeles Lakers. With nine NBA championships, the Lakers attract attention from all over the world. Though crowds are treated to some amazing basketball, cheer fans know the Laker Girls are the main attraction!

Cheering for a high-profile team can often kick-start a career. Just ask former Laker Girls Paula Abdul and Emily Harper. Abdul climbed the pop charts and later judged *American Idol*. Harper lit up the small screen on the soap opera *Passions*. Other Laker Girls are sure to follow in their fancy footsteps.

"Cheer fans know the Laker Girls are the main attraction!"

True Texan Talent

Deep in the heart of Texas is a group of star-spangled sweethearts: the Dallas Cowboys Cheerleaders. These spirited dancers can be spotted by their white cowboy boots and daring blue uniforms.

As one of the NFL's first dance squads, the Dallas Cowboys Cheerleaders have a colorful history and rich tradition. The team has performed around the world and with stars like Beyoncé and Shania Twain.

In 2006 and 2007, the team's tough selection process was featured on a Country Music Television (CMT) reality show. Cheerleaders completed four months of boot-camp-like training. The group was cut from more than 1,000 women to just 36 talented dancers. Talk about survival of the fittest!

Funky Fresh and Supersonic

As the saying goes, "hip-hop, you don't stop." The Seattle Sonics dance team is living proof that hip-hop dancers are indeed unstoppable!

The lights go down at a Seattle Supersonics home game. The floor lights up in a sea of glow sticks. Using shiny props and an upbeat routine, Sonics dancers set the stage for the basketball players' entrance. And the crowd goes wild!

The Sonics' routines depart from the typical jazzy style in favor of an energetic, in-your-face approach. From cool, urban breakdance to edgy, tribal-influenced krumping, the Sonics do it all!

Professional cheerleaders like the Sonics dedicate a ton of time, energy, and hard work to their sport. Remember, every cheerleader has one essential element needed to make it big: spirit. Take a cue from these cutting-edge dancers — push yourself to new limits. You won't get there overnight, but with some real dedication and a ton a spirit, you can achieve your pro-cheer dreams.

GLOSSARY

audition (aw-DISH-uhn) — a performance by a dancer or cheerleader to see whether she or he is suitable for the squad

choreography (kor-ee-OG-ruh-fee) — the creation and arrangement of movements that make up a routine

dunk team (DUHNK TEEM) — a group of athletes who perform choreographed basketball and acrobatic feats

krumping (KRUHMP-ing) — a fast-paced style of hip-hop dancing based on traditional African dance

outreach (OUT-reech) — a program that offers services or assistance to those in need

poise (POIZ) — carrying and presenting yourself with confidence

FAST FACTS

Pro cheerleaders need to know more than just dancing and stunting. Dallas Cowboys Cheerleader hopefuls must pass a written test. The test includes questions about the cheer squad's history, football team, the NFL, and current events. Knowledge is power!

When trying out for a pro squad, your outfit can help you stand out in the crowd. Some girls will spend up to $500 to get the right outfit for an audition.

Many pro squads hold clinics for younger dancers. The pro gals share dance moves, tips, and pro secrets with the younger crowd.

READ MORE

Carrier, Justin, and Donna McKay.
Complete Cheerleading. Champaign, Ill.:
Human Kinetics, 2006.

Jones, Jen. *Cheer Basics: Rules to
Cheer By.* Cheerleading. Mankato, Minn.:
Capstone Press, 2006.

Singer, Lynn. *Cheerleading.* New York:
Rosen, 2007.

INTERNET SITES

FactHound offers a safe,
fun way to find Internet sites
related to this book. All of the
sites on FactHound have been researched by
our staff.

Here's how

1. Visit *www.facthound.com*

2. Choose your grade level.

3. Type in this book ID **1429613491** for
age-appropriate sites. You may also browse
subjects by clicking on letters, or by clicking on
pictures and words.

4. Click on the **Fetch It** button.

FactHound will fetch the best sites for you!

ABOUT THE AUTHOR

While growing up in Ohio, Jen Jones spent seven years as a cheerleader for her grade school and high school squads. (Not surprisingly, she was voted "Most Spirited" several times by her classmates.) Following high school, she became a coach and spurred several cheer teams to competition victory. For two years, she cheered and choreographed on the cheer squad for the Chicago Lawmen, a semi-professional football team.

As well as teaching occasional dance and cheer workshops, Jen now works in sunny Los Angeles as a freelance writer for publications like *American Cheerleader, Cheer Biz News,* and *Dance Spirit.* She is also a member of the Society of Children's Book Writers and Illustrators.

Index